Karen's Promise

Other books by
Ann M. Martin

Leo the Magnificat
Rachel Parker, Kindergarten Show-off
Eleven Kids, One Summer
Ma and Pa Dracula
Yours Turly, Shirley
Ten Kids, No Pets
With You and Without You
Me and Katie (the Pest)
Stage Fright
Inside Out
Bummer Summer

For older readers:

Missing Since Monday
Just a Summer Romance
Slam Book

THE BABY-SITTERS CLUB series
THE BABY-SITTERS CLUB mysteries
THE KIDS IN MS. COLMAN'S CLASS series
BABY-SITTERS LITTLE SISTER series
(see inside book covers for a complete listing)

Little Sister

Karen's Promise
Ann M. Martin

Illustrations by Susan Tang

A
LITTLE APPLE
PAPERBACK

SCHOLASTIC INC.
New York Toronto London Auckland Sydney

The author gratefully acknowledges
Diane Molleson
for her help
with this book.

A Windy Afternoon

"Karen, catch!" Andrew threw his Frisbee high in the air. I almost caught it, but the wind beat me to it. The Frisbee blew out of Daddy's backyard.

"Oh, Andrew," I said. I tried not to sound too impatient. Andrew is my little brother. He is four going on five.

"Don't worry, Karen. I'll find it," said Andrew. He was already running off. I sighed. I did not really want to play Frisbee anyway. It was too windy, and I had a lot to think about.

You are probably wondering who I am. Let me introduce myself. My name is Karen Brewer. I am seven years old. I have long blonde hair and blue eyes. I wear glasses. And this is what I was thinking about.

I just found out that Seth, my stepfather, is moving to Chicago for six months. He made up his mind yesterday. That means Mommy will be moving with him, of course. But I am not sure what is going to happen to Andrew and me.

You see, we do not live with Mommy and Seth all the time. We have two houses: a big house (Daddy's house where we are now) and a little house (Mommy and Seth's). I will explain more about my two houses in a minute.

"Andrew, we need to talk," I announced when I saw him come back with the Frisbee.

"Oh, Karen, let's play some more, please, puh-lease," begged Andrew.

"Andrew," I repeated. "We do have to

talk." (I can sound very firm when I want to.)

Andrew looked down at the grass. "Oh, you mean about Chicago." He did not sound happy.

"Yes," I said. "You know, I do not want Mommy and Seth to move either."

"Do you think Seth will change his mind?" asked Andrew hopefully.

I shook my head. "No. You know Mommy said he is really going." Andrew and I had talked to Mommy on the phone the day before. That is how we learned about Seth's decision. "But it is only for six months," I reminded Andrew.

"I know. But six months is a long time."

I nodded.

"What do you think will happen to us?" asked Andrew in a very small voice.

"I am not sure," I said.

"You aren't?" Andrew looked surprised.

"No. I really do not know if we will go with them or stay here in Stoneybrook.

Mommy said she would tell us more in a couple of days."

"I know," said Andrew.

Andrew clutched his Frisbee. The wind rustled the branches of the trees in Daddy's backyard. Usually the backyard at the big house is fun to play in, but today it looked a little scary. Maybe it was the wind, or the gray clouds that were blocking out the sun.

"Karen," Andrew began. He looked like he was about to start crying. "You won't go anywhere without me, will you?"

I did not want Andrew to be so upset. So I made a promise to him.

"No, Andrew. I will not. I promise that no matter what happens, we will stay together."

Andrew sighed with relief. I was glad he felt better.

"Karen! Karen!"

I turned around to see who was calling me. It was Nannie. (Nannie is my step-grandmother.) She wanted to know if I would help her in the kitchen. She was making chocolate candy.

"Sure!" I called.

"I'm coming too," said Andrew, following me. "I want to lick the bowl."

Two of Everything

Nannie was busy in her kitchen making chocolate-covered marshmallows. She asked me to hand her the ingredients she needed. Andrew sat at the kitchen table watching us. Nannie and I spend many hours in the big house cooking.

Let me tell you a little more about the big house and the little house. First of all, I did not always live in two houses. When I was very little, Andrew and I lived with Mommy and Daddy in the big house here in Stoneybrook, Connecticut. Then Mommy and Daddy started fighting — at first a little, then a lot. Finally they got a divorce. They told Andrew and me they still loved us very much, but they did not love each other anymore. So Mommy moved out of the big house. (Daddy stayed there. It is the house he grew up in.) Mommy moved to a little house, not far away. Then she married Seth. Now he is my stepfather. Daddy married again too. He married Elizabeth, my stepmother.

Andrew and I spend every other month with Daddy in the big house. The rest of the time we live with Mommy in the little house. At least that is what we used to do. Now that Mommy and Seth were going to move, I did not know what would happen.

Here are the people and pets in my little-house family: Mommy, Seth, Andrew, me, Rocky and Midgie (Seth's cat and dog), Emily Junior (my very own rat), and Bob (Andrew's hermit crab).

Here are the people and pets in my big-house family: Daddy, Elizabeth, Kristy, Charlie, Sam, David Michael, Emily Michelle, Nannie, Shannon, Boo-Boo, Goldfishie, Crystal Light the Second, Emily Junior, and Bob. (Emily Junior and Bob go back and forth when Andrew and I do.)

Kristy, Charlie, Sam, and David Michael are Elizabeth's children. (Elizabeth was married once before she married Daddy.) That makes them my stepsister and stepbrothers. Charlie and Sam are old. They go to high school. David Michael is seven, like me. Kristy is one of my favorite people ever. She is thirteen and she runs a baby-sitting business with her friends from school. Emily Michelle is my adopted sister. She is only two years old. (I love her, so I named my pet rat after her.) Daddy and Elizabeth adopted her from the faraway country of Vietnam. Nannie is Elizabeth's mother. She helps take care of the big house and all us kids. The pets too. We have a lot of them. Shannon is David Michael's puppy. Boo-Boo is Daddy's fat old cat. And Goldfishie and Crystal Light the Second are goldfish who belong to Andrew and me.

I made up special nicknames for my brother and me. I call us Andrew Two-Two and Karen Two-Two. (I thought up those names after my teacher read a book to our class. It was called *Jacob Two-Two Meets the Hooded Fang*.) Andrew and I are two-twos because we have two of so many things. We have two houses and two families, two mommies, two daddies, two cats, and two dogs. Plus I have two bicycles, one at each house. And I have two stuffed cats who look exactly alike. Goosie lives at the little house. Moosie stays at the big house. Also, Andrew and I have two sets of clothes, books, and toys. This way, we do not need to pack much when we go back and forth.

I even have a best friend near each house. Hannie Papadakis lives across the street and one house down from Daddy. Nancy Dawes lives next door to Mommy. Hannie, Nancy, and I are all in Ms. Colman's second-grade class at Stoneybrook Academy. I will miss Hannie and Nancy very much if I move. We do everything together. We call ourselves the Three Musketeers.

Being a two-two is hard sometimes. Andrew and I miss the family we are not staying with. But mostly we think we are lucky. So many people care about us. And so many people will miss me if I move to Chicago. Of course, I will miss them a lot too.

Karen in the Kitchen

Nannie seemed busier than usual in her kitchen that day. Nannie makes the most wonderful chocolate I have ever tasted. It is so good, people pay her for it. She has her own business making chocolate candies. She sells them in baskets for gifts or as centerpieces. Best of all, she lets me help her.

Nannie has two kitchens. One is just the regular kitchen where she often cooks meals for my big-house family. She calls the other one her second kitchen. (It used to be the pantry.) And that is where she plans her recipes, keeps her records, and puts together candy baskets for her business.

Today Nannie was trying out a new recipe for chocolate-covered marshmallows. I watched her blend sugar, flour, and milk in a saucepan. I measured the flour.

"Flour?" asked Andrew. "In candy? Where is the chocolate?"

"I'll add the chocolate after all these ingredients are blended," said Nannie. "Don't worry."

After a while Andrew got bored watching Nannie and me measure and stir. Luckily, David Michael asked Andrew to play catch with him.

When Andrew left, I told Nannie about my promise to Andrew. Nannie knew about Seth's news. But she did not know what was going to happen to Andrew and me. (How could she? I did not know yet either.) I do not think she wanted me to go to Chicago. When I finished telling her about my promise, she looked sort of sad.

"What would you like to do, Karen?" she asked me.

I sighed and watched her put some butter in the saucepan. "I really do not know," I said. "I mean, Chicago is big and exciting. At least that is what Mommy said. But I will miss Stoneybrook, and you, and everyone else here."

Nannie sighed too. "I will certainly miss Andrew and you," she said. "And I will miss all the help you give me in the kitchen."

"Really?" I asked. I stood up a little straighter.

"Yes," said Nannie. "You are a big help to me, you know."

I beamed. I am very proud of Nannie and her business. "I hope Andrew and I do not have to leave Stoneybrook."

"Well, whatever happens, remember it is only for six months," said Nannie.

"That is what I tried to tell Andrew," I said. "But six months seems like forever."

"I know," said Nannie. She was chopping some nuts into tiny pieces. "Karen, would you hand me more nuts?" I did. I also stirred chocolate and butter over the stove. I was very careful.

"Karen, in all the excitement, I did not tell you my news yet."

I stopped stirring to look at her. "Is it good news?" I asked.

"Yes, it is," said Nannie, smiling. "I have just received my first big order. I will be making candy basket centerpieces for the hospital. They are having a big dinner at the end of the month to raise money."

"Oh, Nannie. That is wonderful," I said. I gave her a big hug.

Nannie laughed. "Keep stirring the chocolate," she reminded me.

"Oh, right. Are we making all these marshmallow chocolates for the hospital?" I asked. I was hoping there would be some extras for the family.

"Yes indeed."

Darn, I thought to myself.

"Wow, something sure smells good," said Kristy as she came in the kitchen. She

walked to the stove to see what I was stirring. Kristy loves to taste everything we cook.

"It is candy for a dinner at the hospital," I said. "It is Nannie's first really big order."

"I know," said Kristy, smiling. "I overhead you talking about it when I came in the house."

I laughed. The big house is very big. But it seems small sometimes because so many people live here.

The Big Meeting

A few days later, when I came home from school, guess what I saw? Mommy's car.

"Andrew, Andrew, Mommy's here!" I yelled. Andrew was outside playing. When he heard me calling, he rushed inside.

Mommy and Seth were in the front hall talking to Daddy, Nannie, and Elizabeth. Andrew ran right into Mommy's arms. I gave Seth a big hug. (I miss them when I am at the big house.)

Everyone was talking at once. I was asking about Rocky and Midgie. Andrew was telling Mommy about a turtle he found in the backyard. And the grown-ups were talking to each other about where to hold the meeting.

"What meeting?" I asked. Suddenly I realized today must be special because Elizabeth was home from work early. (Daddy works at home most of the time so I was not surprised to see him.)

"A meeting about Chicago," answered Mommy. "Remember, I said Seth and I would be here to discuss our plans with you in person."

I remembered. I also started to feel a little nervous. What plans was she talking about?

"We can all go into the dining room," Daddy was saying.

Soon Elizabeth, Daddy, Mommy, Seth, Andrew, and I were all sitting around the big table. Everyone looked serious. I gulped.

Daddy cleared his throat. Andrew squirmed in his chair. I wished Daddy would hurry up and tell us what was going to happen to Andrew and me. Instead Daddy looked at Mommy.

Mommy began talking. "Your father and I have decided that Andrew will move to Chicago with Seth and me."

I looked at Andrew. Andrew's eyes looked very round. "What about Karen?" he asked.

Everyone was looking at me now. "Karen will decide for herself what she wants to do," said Daddy.

"You mean, I can stay in Stoneybrook if I want?" (I could not believe it.)

The grown-ups nodded.

"But Karen," Andrew protested.

"I did not say I was going to stay," I told Andrew. "I was just asking."

"You don't have to make a decision right away," said Seth. "We will not be moving until the middle of next month."

"That's right," said Mommy. "So take time to think things over and decide what you really want to do."

Daddy agreed. "We do not necessarily want to take you away from your friends and school in the middle of the term. That is why we thought it would be best if you made this decision yourself."

I nodded. I felt proud that everyone trusted me enough to make my own decision. But it was a gigundoly big decision.

I looked at Andrew. He kept staring at me. I knew he wanted me to tell everyone I was going to Chicago with him. But I needed to think some more. I sighed. This was not going to be easy.

The Three Musketeers
Forever

After the meeting, I ran to the phone in the kitchen. I needed to talk to Hannie and Nancy.

"Hello," I said to Nancy when she picked up the phone. "Can you come over right away?" (I made sure to say *right away* very clearly.)

"What is wrong?" asked Nancy. I guess I sounded upset.

"I have to tell you in person."

"All right. But I have to ask my mother if I can come over."

Nancy's mother said she could visit and that she would drive her.

Hannie ran across the street as soon as we had talked. In fact, she arrived just as Mommy and Seth were getting ready to leave.

" 'Bye, Mommy," I said, hugging her. " 'Bye, Seth." I gave him a hug too. I felt a little sad to see them go. So did Andrew. When he said good-bye to Mommy, he rested his head on her shoulder. I was glad Mommy and Seth were taking Andrew to Chicago. He would be lost without Mommy. But I am older. I do not need Mommy as much as he does. At least, I do not think I do.

Hannie, Andrew, and I waved good-bye as Seth's car pulled out of the driveway. We did not have to wait long for Nancy. Her mother's car passed Seth's at the end of the driveway.

"Nancy!" I shrieked, even though I had just seen her at school.

"Karen!" Nancy shrieked back. Mrs. Dawes laughed. "I will pick you up in an hour," she called to Nancy as she drove away.

An hour. I guessed that was enough time. I grabbed Nancy's hand and Hannie's arm. "Come to the backyard where we can talk," I said.

I led them to my favorite spot — underneath the lilac bushes. The lilacs were not in bloom yet, but I did not care. We sat on a stone bench, and I told them about the family meeting. (Hannie and Nancy already knew Seth and Mommy were moving to Chicago for six months. But they did not know this latest news.)

"So, you can stay here if you want to," said Hannie when I finished talking. She was beaming.

I nodded. "But I promised Andrew that we would stay together, no matter what happened."

"You did?" my friends said together. They did not look happy.

I nodded and sighed. For once I could not think of anything else to say.

"Oh, Karen," said Hannie. "You cannot leave! We do everything together."

"Yeah," said Nancy. She twisted her pink plastic ring around her finger. "We're the Three Musketeers. Remember?"

"Of course I remember," I said. (What was Nancy thinking?)

"So, you just have to tell Andrew that you have to stay here with us," insisted Nancy.

Hannie nodded. "He will understand," she said.

I thought about my promise to Andrew and shook my head. "No, I do not think he will," I said. "Andrew is expecting me to go with him."

"Oh, Karen," wailed Hannie. Nancy looked miserable.

"But, guess what?" I said.

My friends looked at me. "What?" they asked at the same time.

"I still have not decided for sure," I said. "And I do not have to decide right away. So we will still be together for another month — at least."

Recess

"You are it!" I said as I tagged Hannie on the shoulder. Then I ran as fast as I could toward the tallest oak tree in the playground. I did not want Hannie to catch me.

Hannie tagged Omar Harris on the arm. He ran to the swings and tagged Sara Ford.

"But I am not playing," Sara protested.

"You are now!" shouted Omar as he dashed away.

Sara laughed and ran after him. "I will get you for this," she said. But Omar was too quick for her. She tagged Bobby Gianelli, who runs a lot more slowly than Omar. Bobby used to be the class bully, but he is okay now, most of the time. He was mad about being tagged by a girl, though. He chased Sara to the slides, around the sandbox, and over to the oak tree.

Oops. Guess what happened?

Bobby tagged me. I was so busy watching, I forgot to run. And Sara was too quick for him. I was it — again.

I looked around the playground. All of the kids in my class were there. Pamela Harding was sitting on a bench with her friends, Leslie Morris and Jannie Gilbert. Pamela is my best enemy. Pamela and her friends hardly ever play with us at recess. They think games like tag are for babies. They would rather sit and talk and not mess up their clothes.

The twins, Tammi and Terry Barkan, were on the slides. Natalie Springer was pushing Audrey Green on the swings. Everyone else was playing tag.

Addie Sidney zoomed past me in her

wheelchair. Hank Lamar and Ricky Torres were headed toward the oak tree. I decided to chase after them. I tagged Hank instead of Ricky. (Ricky is my pretend husband, and it is not good for wives to tag their husbands.)

"Oh, *Karen!*" said Hank when I caught him on the shoulder. But he did not look too mad. He started to chase Nancy, but stopped suddenly. In fact, almost everyone in my class stopped playing all at once.

Some grown-ups were walking across the playground. They were carrying boxes that were covered in foil. I knew that there was going to be a bake sale today. So I could guess what was in the boxes.

We all rushed over to talk to the grown-ups.

"Do you have any brownies in there?" I asked. "How about chocolate chip cookies?"

"Cool!" shouted Hank. "Can we buy some now?"

One of the grown-ups had some very bad news. "I am sorry," she said. "But our bake sale does not start until after school. We are just bringing the boxes inside right now."

"I guess we will have to wait until later," said Pamela. "But I will be the first person at the bake sale after school."

Then Ms. Colman (our gigundoly wonderful teacher) announced that recess was over. Boo and bullfrogs!

"I bet those brownies do not taste nearly as good as Nannie's candy," I muttered to Hannie as we walked back to our classroom.

Paris, New York, or Chicago

My class could not settle down after recess.

I took my seat in the front row. Ricky sits on one side of me. (It is good that husbands and wives can sit together.) Natalie sits on my other side. We are all in the front row because we wear glasses.

"All right, class," said Ms. Colman. "Before you take out your geography workbooks, I have an announcement to make."

Oh, goody. I love Ms. Colman's Surprising Announcements.

"As you know, class, we are going to spend this month studying cities," continued Ms. Colman.

I nodded. I knew we were coming to the unit on cities in our social studies books.

"We will begin with a special group project. Each group will study one city and will prepare a report on that city to present to the class." Ms. Colman stopped talking and looked around the room.

"Can we pick the city we want to study?" I asked. I was so excited that I forgot to raise my hand first. Ms. Colman does not like it when we call out in class. But she smiled at me anyway. (See what a wonderful teacher she is?)

"Yes, Karen. Each group may decide which city to study. But I would like you to pick a large city. Your book gives you some suggestions."

"I want to study Chicago," I blurted out. "Chicago is a large city."

This time Ms. Colman reminded me not

to call out in class. But she did not look mad.

"You have to decide that with your group, Karen," Ricky reminded me.

"That is correct," said Ms. Colman. "Now, class, I have chosen the groups and I will write them on the board. Wait until I finish writing, then quietly join your group."

I turned the pages of my book while Ms. Colman wrote on the board. I saw pictures and names of lots of cities I had heard of: Beijing, Bogotá, Stockholm. . . .

Ricky tapped me on the arm. "Karen, we're in the same group," he told me.

I looked at the board. I was in a group with Ricky, Nancy, and Natalie. Hooray. I liked everyone in my group.

That is, I liked them until we started arguing about what city we were going to study. Nancy wanted Paris. She loves ballet and she said lots of famous dancers studied in Paris. Ricky only wanted New York. Natalie Springer did not really care, but she thought

Paris or New York sounded better than Chicago.

"Why Chicago?" Ricky asked me for what seemed like the hundredth time since we had joined our groups.

I shrugged. I did not want my whole class to know I might be moving. I know it is bad to keep secrets from your husband. But I could not help it. "I might be going there for a visit soon," was all I said.

"Really?" said Ricky. Nancy gave me a funny look.

Natalie opened her eyes wider. "You should have told us that before," she said.

I shrugged again. "Look. Chicago has one of the tallest buildings in the world. Taller than the twin towers in New York."

"Hmm," said Ricky. He looked sort of interested. I told Nancy Chicago has a famous ballet company too. (I hoped I was right.) And I told Natalie about Chicago's world-famous aquarium, since Natalie likes animals of all kinds.

"How come you know so much about Chicago?" Ricky wanted to know.

"Uh, my stepfather has been telling me about it," I answered.

My group asked me some more questions. Finally they said Chicago would be okay.

"Very well," said Ms. Colman when we told her what our choice was. "No one else has chosen that city."

That was a relief. I really wanted to learn about Chicago, since I might move there.

Before we left for the day, Ms. Colman made another announcement. "I am working on a fund-raiser, a project to raise money for Stoneybrook Manor," she said. (Stoneybrook Manor is a place where senior citizens live. My class knew all about it because we once "adopted" some of the people there as extra grandparents.) "I am going to host a dinner at the manor. I will sell tickets. And I will give the ticket money to the manor. Please tell your parents about this event."

I waved my hand in the air. I had the best idea.

"Yes, Karen?"

"Will you have candy at your dinner?" I asked. I told everyone about Nannie's business, and how she makes excellent chocolate candy.

"Karen, you are sooo lucky," said Bobby.

"Yeah," said Omar. "You get to eat home-made candy all the time."

Ms. Colman told me that she thought having candy baskets at her dinner might be a good idea. And she would think about hiring Nannie to make them. I was thrilled. I could not wait to tell Nannie.

More Work for Nannie

I rushed home as soon as school was over. I found Nannie in the kitchen giving Andrew, Emily Michelle, and David Michael an after-school snack. (Emily Michelle does not go to school, but she always has an after-school snack with us anyway.) They were eating cupcakes and drinking milk. I grabbed a cupcake with pink icing on it.

"Guess what?" I said to Nannie after my first bite.

"What?" asked Nannie, sounding a little tired. She was looking at the clock.

"Ms. Colman is having a big dinner to raise money for Stoneybrook Manor."

Nannie looked at me. "Yes?"

"Well, she needs someone to make candy baskets. I told her about your business. She will probably call you, if she decides to have candy at her dinner. And I think she will, because she liked my idea." I was talking very fast, since I was excited.

I thought Nannie would be thrilled. But she did not look thrilled. Or even happy. Her shoulders drooped. Her voice sounded tired. "Karen," she began. "I have so much work right now, I do not even know where to start."

I gulped.

Just then, Sam and Kristy walked into the kitchen. "What's the matter, Nannie?" asked Kristy.

"This hospital fund-raiser is taking up more time than I thought," said Nannie. "And on top of that, I am trying to make baskets for Easter. And now I may be making candy baskets for Karen's teacher."

"It is great that your new company is getting all this business," said Kristy. (Kristy would say that. She loves all the business her baby-sitting club gets.)

"I know," said Nannie. "I suppose I should be grateful. But I am a little worried about filling all my orders on time."

"Well, we can help you," said Kristy. "Right?" She looked at each of us.

"Right," we said.

Kristy found a notebook and started writing things down. "Now, let me see. Charlie has a car. He can deliver your orders." (Charlie was not around, but I did not think he would mind. He gives all of us rides in his old car. He calls it the Junk Bucket.) "And Karen, Sam, David Michael, and I can help you make your chocolate."

"Sure," I said. The others nodded.

"What about me?" asked Andrew.

"Meee, meeee," echoed Emily Michelle.

"Hmm," said Kristy. She tapped her pencil on the notepad. "You two can be Nannie's official tasters. You will sample

everything we make to make sure it tastes all right."

"Sure!" shouted Andrew. Emily beamed.

"All right, we are in business," said Kristy.

"I guess we are," said Nannie. But she still looked worried.

School Lunch

"Gross. Mystery meat again," muttered Bobby Gianelli.

I turned to look at him. (I was at the head of the lunch line.) "Shh," I warned. "The cook will hear you."

"I do not care," said Bobby. "Maybe if he hears me, he will stop serving such gross food."

"I do not think it is so bad," I said. I held out my plate for the lunch, which happened to be meat loaf. It came with mashed potatoes and corn. Bobby looked at my plate and rolled his eyes.

"You know, Karen, I really wish you would bring in some of your grandmother's candy."

"Yeah," said Hank, who was behind Bobby. "We could use some good food around here."

I frowned. Luckily, the cafeteria ladies ignored them.

"I will try to," I said. "But my grandmother is very busy with her business right now." In fact, Nannie had been too busy to pack my lunch that morning.

"Oh, Karen," said Hank. "Please?"

"I will see," I said as I walked to a table near the window. I saved seats for Hannie and Nancy.

Just then Ricky walked by with his tray. "Karen," he said. "I heard you are moving to Chicago."

"You are moving away?" asked Chris, who was behind Ricky.

"No!" I said crossly. "I mean, if I do move, it will only be for six months. But I am not sure I am going at all."

Darn. I did not want the whole school to know.

"I am sorry I told some kids," said Nancy when we were eating. "I did not think it was a secret."

"Well, it is not really a secret," I replied.

"And you may not really be moving," said Hannie.

I nodded. "I have not decided what I will do," I said. I took a bite of meat loaf. It did not taste too bad.

"Try to stay, Karen. Please," said Nancy.

"Yes," said Hannie.

"I would like to," I said. "Even if I have to eat this cafeteria food every day." I waved my forkful of mashed potatoes in the air.

We all laughed.

Too Many Cooks

"I am home," I called loudly when I came into the kitchen after school.

"Indoor voice, Karen. We hear you," called Nannie. But she was laughing. Most of my family was already helping Nannie in the kitchen. Kristy was stirring a vat of chocolate on the stove. Sam was shelling peanuts. David Michael was measuring sugar into a bowl, except he was spilling a lot of it.

"David Michael, pay attention," I said. "You are wasting sugar."

"Karen, stop being so bossy." David Michael looked up and glared at me. More sugar spilled on the counter.

"I am not being bossy."

"Yes you are. You think you are the boss of the world."

"I do not."

"Do too."

"All right, you two," said Nannie. She wiped her hands on her apron and told me to help Kristy by the stove. Then she told David Michael to be more careful. (Hmmph.) "I have to check on Emily Michelle," Nannie said as she left the room.

I watched Kristy stir the chocolate. It smelled sooo good. I wanted to taste some. But Kristy told me I could not. It was too hot. And it would not be sanitary (that was Kristy's word) for me to dip my fingers in it. Instead I decided to tell Kristy a riddle from a book I just read. It was called *A Little Book of Animal Riddles* by Jim Murphy.

"Why did the elephant run away from the circus?" I asked.

"I give up," said Kristy. She did not even look at me.

"Because he was tired of working for peanuts."

"Oh, Karen," said Kristy.

"I know another," I said. This time David Michael, Sam, and Kristy all stopped what they were doing to listen to me. (I love an audience.)

"Why do little pigs eat so much?" I asked. I snorted a little, for effect.

The others were quiet.

"They want to make hogs of themselves," Sam finally answered.

Everyone laughed, except me. "How did you know that?" I asked.

"It is an old joke," answered Sam.

"It is funny," said David Michael, laughing. He was waving his measuring spoon in the air, and he knocked over a bag of flour, which spilled on the floor, making clouds of fine white dust.

"Oh, no," said David Michael. Sam grabbed a broom and started sweeping. "Get a mop and some water," he told David Michael.

"Kristy, the chocolate smells like it's burning!" I shouted.

"Oh my gosh," said Kristy. She began stirring the chocolate again — very quickly. But it was too late.

"You have to keep stirring it all the time," Nannie told Kristy firmly when she returned.

Kristy nodded. I could tell she felt bad.

Nannie shook her head and looked around the kitchen. Kristy was taking the burned chocolate off the stove. Sam was making flour swirl in the air with his broom. David Michael was mopping after him, but the water was turning the flour into a paste. Dirty bowls, mixing spoons, and peanut shells were piled on the counters.

"At this rate, we will never have the baskets finished in time," said Nannie.

No one said anything, not even me. Our first day working together had been a disaster. I had promised to help Nannie, not make her job harder. I hoped things would get better.

The Great Fire

"Nancy, pass me more loose-leaf paper, please," I said.

"Look, here is a great picture book about Chicago," said Natalie.

"Another one?" asked Ricky, looking up from his stack of books.

My class was very busy. We had spent a lot of time in the school library. And we had checked out plenty of books. Now we were sitting in our classroom, in our groups. And we were trying to organize our information.

Ricky was reading about the famous

buildings in Chicago. Nancy was reading about Chicago's history. And Natalie was telling me about Chicago's museums. "Chicago has one of the biggest aquariums in the world," she was saying. "And in one museum you can explore a real coal mine."

"Cool," I said.

I was looking through a book about Chicago's Great Fire. "Did you know that in eighteen seventy-one, almost all of Chicago burned down from a fire that started in a barn?" I asked my group.

"Oh, yeah, I know about the Great Fire," said Ricky. "Almost all the buildings were made of wood then. That is why the city burned so fast."

"But people got together and rebuilt the whole city," I said. "And they made sure to use stone in many of the new buildings, not wood."

Ricky nodded.

"You know, I have a lot of books about Chicago's Great Fire," I said, pointing to my stack.

"I do not think we will have trouble finding things to talk about," said Natalie.

"How are you coming along?" asked Ms. Colman. She sat down in an empty chair next to Ricky. (She was visiting all the groups to see how they were doing.)

"Oh, fine," said Ricky. "We may have too many things to talk about."

Ms. Colman laughed. "It is better to have too much material than too little," she said. "I am sure you will find a good way to organize your presentation."

"I hope so," said Nancy. She looked up from her book about Chicago's history.

"Oh, by the way, Karen," said Ms. Colman. "I called your grandmother about making candy baskets for the fund-raiser. She said she would do it."

"Oh, goody," I said. "I am helping her, you know."

Ms. Colman smiled and stood up to leave our group. "I am sure you are a big help to her," she said.

"You know how to make candy?" Ricky asked me.

"Well, sort of," I said. "I am just learning."

"Could you bring in some samples?" asked Natalie.

"Uh, maybe," I replied.

"Oh, Karen, please," begged Nancy. "Your house always smells so good when Nannie is making her chocolate. I've always wanted to taste some."

I sighed.

"Please, Karen," said Natalie. "Just little samples for our group."

"Yeah," said Ricky.

"Oh, all right," I finally said. "But do not tell the other kids about this."

"Don't tell us what?" asked Hannie, who was sitting nearby.

"Nothing," I said.

"Karen, tell me," insisted Hannie. "The Three Musketeers never keep secrets from each other."

Hannie was right. I promised her a sample of candy too. Then I had to promise candy to the other kids in Hannie's group: Bobby, Addie, and Audrey. (I had already sort of promised candy to Bobby and Hank anyway.) Pamela overheard me talking to Audrey, and she wanted candy too. So did the twins. So did Ian, Sara, and Omar. Before I left for the day, I had promised candy to everyone in my class.

Nannie was going to be very mad.

Shopping

Guess what? I did not have a chance to tell Nannie about candy for my class that afternoon.

I rushed home to help her. But Nannie did not want me in the kitchen. She said there were too many cooks the day before. Today Sam and David Michael were helping. Nannie wanted Kristy and me to go shopping for some decorations for the baskets.

Oh goody, I thought. (I do love to cook, but I also love to shop.)

Kristy looked happy too. (She does not enjoy cooking very much.)

"Here," said Nannie, handing Kristy a list of things to buy and some money. "You can probably find most of these supplies at a candy store."

"Really?" Kristy sounded surprised.

"Oh yes. Candy makers often sell decorations and supplies."

"Cool," said Kristy as she put on her jacket.

I wanted to go to Polly's. (That is a famous, old-fashioned candy store in downtown Stoneybrook.) But Kristy said it was too far away for us to walk.

"You know," I said as I skipped along beside Kristy, "I will really miss you if I move to Chicago."

"I will really miss you too, Karen. Are you moving for sure?"

"No. But I may have to, because I promised Andrew we would stay together, no matter what."

"Oh," said Kristy in a quiet voice. "I did

not know about your promise to Andrew. That was a big promise, Karen."

I stopped skipping and looked down at the sidewalk. (I knew it was a big promise. I did not want to think about it.)

"Cheer up," said Kristy, grabbing my hand. "Let's forget about Chicago this afternoon."

I thought that was a great idea. And you know what? We had the best time shopping. First we went to a candy store that had baskets full of four-leaf clovers and leprechauns in the window for St. Patrick's Day.

"Does Nannie want to decorate her baskets like that?" I asked.

Kristy looked at the list. "I do not think so," she said.

In the store, Kristy asked the man behind the counter for colored foil, candy cups, cellophane, and ribbon.

I walked around the store. The woman at the cash register asked me if I wanted a free sample.

"Sure," I said.

"Choose the one you would like."

I looked at all the candy behind the counter. I saw chocolate-covered pretzels, chocolate strawberries, peanut bars, lemon drops, almond bark, caramels, and peppermints.

"Um, I will have a chocolate-covered strawberry, please," I said politely.

It was not bad. But Nannie's Chocolate Magic is much better. (That is Nannie's special chocolate coating for dipping fruits. She invented the recipe and won an important cooking contest with it too.)

Next we went into a store that sold a little of everything. "Nannie said we could be creative," said Kristy, waving her list. "She needs some things to put in the baskets with the candy. Now, what would be good to put in the baskets for the hospital?"

Hmmm. I was thinking. "What about mugs?" I suggested.

"Too expensive," said Kristy.

We bought lollipops, colored bows, and leaves made from fabric.

"Nannie is going to have the prettiest baskets ever," I said as we were walking home.

Kristy smiled at me. "Definitely," she said.

No Extras

"What did you buy?" asked David Michael when he saw our bags.

"Lots of good stuff," said Kristy, opening one of her bags to show him.

Nannie barely glanced at us when we came in. She seemed frazzled. (That is a word Sam says a lot.) When I looked around the kitchen, I saw why. Sam and David Michael were at the sink cleaning up a big bowl of something that looked like glue.

"We ruined a batch of chocolate by adding cornstarch instead of flour," Sam explained.

"I accidentally handed Sam the cornstarch," said David Michael. "It looks a lot like flour."

I thought David Michael was very careless in the kitchen. But I decided not to say anything. Instead, I asked Nannie if she wanted to see what we had bought.

Nannie did not answer. She looked up and rubbed her eyes. "Oh, my goodness, what time is it?" she asked.

"Quarter to six," answered Kristy, looking at her watch.

Nannie sighed. "So late, already. I have not finished making these coconut bars. And it is already dinnertime."

"We will help," said Kristy. "I can give Emily her supper and put her to bed for you."

"And we can help you make dinner," said Elizabeth, who had just come into the kitchen. She was still carrying her briefcase. Elizabeth is very organized, like Kristy. She set down her briefcase and put a big pot of water on the stove for spaghetti.

Emily Michelle was eating graham crackers with Andrew underneath the kitchen table. Cracker crumbs were everywhere: in their hair, their clothes, all over the floor and kitchen chairs.

"Andrew," I said. (I tried to say his name like Mommy does when she is mad.)

"Oh, Emily," said Kristy, shaking her head.

"We were playing house," said Andrew.

"You were making a mess," I said. I helped Kristy clean it up. So did Andrew.

"Did you taste some of Nannie's chocolate?" I asked Andrew while we were sweeping. (It is a good thing there are a lot of brooms in the big house.)

"No, I did not," said Andrew. "David Michael said there was not enough for us to taste."

"He's right," said Sam, who was drying the mixing bowl. "Between what David

Michael and I tasted or ruined, there was barely enough left for Nannie's cooking."

Darn, I thought. At this rate there will not be any extras for my class.

I looked at Nannie. She was busy washing some big mixing spoons. This was not a good time to tell her about the candy I had promised to my class. I did not know when would be a good time.

I had a lot of problems.

An Accident

The next day at school, I was hoping no one would ask me about the candy. But of course everyone did. I had not even sat down when Ricky asked me where his candy was. That reminded Natalie to ask about hers. Then while Ms. Colman was teaching us fractions, I received a note. It read:

> Dear Karen,
>   Did you bring our candy?
>   We are hungry and cannot wait!
>
>   Your friends, Pamela, Leslie, and Jannie

I did not answer their silly note. They would have to be patient. For heaven's sake.

"Nannie is very busy right now. You will have to wait for your candy," I politely told all the kids who asked. I had to tell Ricky twice because he asked twice.

That afternoon I went right home to talk to Nannie. She was wrapping bars of chocolate with gold foil. Kristy was playing with Andrew and Emily Michelle in the small kitchen. Sam was separating eggs. Charlie was using the electric mixer. It made so much noise, no one could hear me.

"CAN YOU STOP THE MIXER?" I shouted to Charlie.

"WHAT?"

"I HAVE TO TALK TO NANNIE!" (No one even told me to use my indoor voice.)

"LATER," shouted Charlie. "WE HAVE TO FINISH WHIPPING THESE EGG WHITES."

I went outside to play ball with Hannie.

When I came back, Sam and Charlie were talking to Nannie. They did not want to be interrupted.

I sighed. It seemed as if I would never have the chance to ask Nannie about candy for my class.

"Have you talked to Andrew yet?" Nancy asked me one afternoon when we were skipping rope in Hannie's backyard.

"Um, no," I admitted.

"Are you going to Chicago?"

"I do not know." I tripped and became tangled in my jump rope. I did not want to think about Chicago. I just wanted to play with my friends.

"Oh, Karen, you promised us you would try to stay in Stoneybrook," said Hannie.

"I know," I replied. *Skip, skip, skip.* "I will talk to Andrew." *Skip, skip, skip.*

"When?" asked Nancy. She had stopped skipping rope.

"Soon," I said. *Skip, skip, skip.*

* * *

At school the kids asked me about Nannie's candy almost every day. Only Hannie and Nancy did not. That is because they are my best friends. And they knew I had not talked to Nannie yet. They also knew Nannie was overworked.

"I told you, Nannie is very busy. You will have to wait for your candy," I repeated to Pamela and Jannie at recess.

"You say that almost every day," said Pamela.

"That is because Nannie is still busy," I said firmly as I walked away.

That afternoon I tried again to talk to Nannie. She was stirring a large vat of chocolate on the stove. Sam and David Michael were in the kitchen with her. Kristy was playing with Andrew and Emily Michelle in the family room. As usual, everyone looked as though they had too much to do. David Michael was stirring something (and spilling a lot of it), and Sam was chopping walnuts.

"Nannie, can I talk to you?" I asked.

Nannie did not even turn around.

"I am very busy, Karen." Nannie sounded tired. (I missed my talks in the kitchen with Nannie, when the two of us were making candy together.) "By the way, I just found out that Ms. Colman's fund-raiser is on the same night as the hospital's," added Nannie.

"It is?" I said.

"Yes. I almost did not accept Ms. Colman's order when I heard that. But I hate to turn away business when I am just getting started."

"This means," said Sam as he handed the nuts to David Michael, "things are going to be even crazier around here."

Nannie nodded grimly and turned around to give instructions to Sam. And to tell David Michael to be more careful. Andrew raced into the kitchen to ask if anyone had seen his Frisbee. Kristy was right behind him. I am not sure what happened after that, because I was looking at Andrew. But suddenly Kristy screamed.

The hot vat of chocolate had been turned over. "Get out of the way!" Kristy cried.

Luckily Nannie did. The vat made a loud thud as it fell. We stared at the thick pools of chocolate that were streaming down the stove and covering the floor.

Time-out

At first no one moved (except to step out of the way of the chocolate).

"Time-out," called Nannie. She turned off the stove.

"What is going on in here?" asked Daddy as he hurried into the kitchen. "I heard some screaming. Is everyone all right?"

"I accidentally knocked over the vat when I turned away from the stove," said Nannie. "I was trying to do too many things at once. No one is hurt."

"That is good," said Daddy. He side-stepped a stream of chocolate.

Nannie grabbed a mop. Sam and Daddy found cloths. Kristy filled up a big bucket of water and handed Andrew and me some sponges. We worked and worked. I think I must have emptied ten pails of chocolate water. When the floor and stove were clean, Nannie suggested we all sit down at the kitchen table and talk. By now Charlie and Elizabeth had returned home too.

"Things are just too crazy around here," said Nannie when we were sitting down.

That is for sure, I thought. But I did not say anything. Everyone nodded, though, which meant they thought so too.

I looked at my big-house family. Almost everyone seemed tired and grumpy. Making chocolate was more work than any of us had imagined. Kristy had had to give up some baby-sitting jobs. Sam was missing baseball practice, and I was not getting to play with Hannie and Nancy very much.

Nannie was telling us how much she appreciated all the help we had given her. But we needed to slow down and be more careful about what we were doing.

I looked at David Michael when Nannie talked about being more careful. Then I remembered I had spilled salt and sugar the day before. Worse than that, I had added salt when I should have added sugar. Nannie was right. We were all working so fast that we were not paying attention.

"I took on too much business too quickly," Nannie was saying. "But I cannot cancel any orders on such short notice."

"So," said Elizabeth, "we, as a family, need to organize ourselves."

"Right," said Kristy. Everyone had a lot of ideas about that. Here are some things we decided:

1) Nannie would have only two helpers in the kitchen at any time. Elizabeth made up a list of when each of us would work.

2) People could not go racing into the

pantry all day long to ask Nannie questions. She needed to concentrate.

3) Daddy and Elizabeth would cook all the family meals until Nannie's orders were filled.

4) Charlie would be available to do the food shopping.

5) We would forget about cooking anything more tonight and go out to dinner. (Everyone really liked that idea.)

New York, San Francisco, or Chicago

On the day of our presentation I had butterflies in my stomach. I had spent so much time helping Nannie that I did not feel ready. Luckily, Natalie, Ricky, and Nancy were going to give the presentation with me, so I would have to talk for only a few minutes. I just hoped I had enough to say (though that is not usually a problem for me).

The first report was about New York. Omar talked about the city's early history. Leslie told us about Central Park. And Pamela went on and on about the great department stores. I felt a little jealous that I was not giving that part of their presentation, because I love to shop in New York City too. Then Hank finished up with a gigundoly cool imaginary trip on the subways.

Next we heard about San Francisco from Hannie, Addie, Bobby, and Audrey. They talked about how it started as a Spanish mission. They also told us about the great earthquake and the Golden Gate Bridge and other stuff. Yikes. Our turn was next.

Natalie took her notes to the front of the room and began. She explained that Chicago is an Indian name and that the city started as a trading post and fort. When she sat down, Ricky told how the railroads helped make the city grow. He also talked a lot about Chicago's buildings. He was making Chicago sound very interesting. I was beginning to think I would like to visit it and see the buildings Ricky was talking about. But I still was not sure I wanted to live there for six whole months.

After Ricky finished, it was my turn. As soon as I started reading from my notes I felt better. I talked about the Great Fire of 1871, how it started in Mrs. O'Leary's barn and spread very fast because of wind (Chicago is called the Windy City) and because most houses, buildings, sidewalks, and even streets were made of wood then. Thousands of people lost their homes and hundreds died, but the city was soon rebuilt and steps were taken to prevent any more big fires.

Instead of not having enough to say, I went on a little too long. Nancy had to rush her talk on the museums to keep our group within our time limit. Then the last two groups gave their presentations on Philadelphia and Seattle. I was so relieved to be done with our report that I did not listen very closely.

The presentations were over. But I still had to talk to Nannie about the candy I had promised my class. And decide about Chicago. Boo and bullfrogs.

Nannie's Plan

As soon as I got home, I went to the kitchen to talk to Nannie. For once, no one else was with her. She was at the stove, stirring a pot of chocolate. I sat down calmly. (I was careful not to break Rule #2.)

"Nannie," I said, "I need to talk to you."

"What about?" Nannie was smiling. "Are you worried about something?"

"Sort of. You see, I was talking to the kids at school, and . . ."

"Yes? What about?"

"Well, I was telling them about the

candy we are making, and . . ."

"And?" Nannie did not look up from the stove.

"And, um, some of them really wanted to have a little of it to taste." I was feeling more and more ashamed. Just then the timer rang. (Whew.) Nannie lifted the pot off the hot burner and onto a cold one. Then she looked at me. "What did you tell them, Karen?"

I looked down. "I promised them I would bring in some chocolate. Only a little, just to taste."

"How many kids did you promise this to?" asked Nannie, her hands on her hips.

"Well, most of the class," I said. I felt as if I were about to start crying.

"That would mean the whole class, since it wouldn't be fair to leave anyone out. Karen, you know how busy I am. I can barely keep up with the orders I have. I do not have time to make *extra* chocolate."

I began to cry a little. I could not help it. "I am sorry, Nannie. I will tell them they cannot have any. They will be mad. But that is all right. It is my fault. I should have asked you first."

Nannie put her hand on my shoulder. "Oh, Karen. Maybe we can find a way to make a *little* something for them. It is out of the question until the big jobs are finished, but if your friends can wait . . ."

"Oh, Nannie, really?"

"Really. If you help me every day with my orders. Then, when I am done, the two of us can make some chocolates for your class."

"Nannie, that would be wonderful!" I said, hugging her around the waist. "Could we make candy baskets for them?"

"Not baskets for everyone, but maybe a few baskets to share."

"That would be great! I will give up playing with Hannie and Nancy until your orders are filled. I will not even talk to them on the phone. I will help you every afternoon and on weekends."

"And you will listen carefully to everything I tell you to do," added Nannie.

I nodded.

"And," said Nannie, "when I already have two helpers in the kitchen, you will wash the dishes and not distract my helpers."

I nodded again.

"Okay. Go wash your hands and put on my spare apron. You can start by measuring out some sugar for me."

Nannie and I worked very hard. It is a good thing I was helping every afternoon. Even though Nannie had two helpers in the kitchen every day, there was always something for me to do.

I learned how to make fudge, how to separate eggs, how to make chocolate leaves. (We used a special brush to paint fabric leaves with chocolate. Then, when the chocolate had set, Nannie peeled the fabric away from the chocolate. The leaves were beautiful.)

Together, Nannie and I made truffles. (Those are fancy chocolates with all different kinds of fillings.) We also made nutty chocolate bars, chocolate cherries, chocolate nuts, chocolate marshmallow nut fudge, coconut bars covered with chocolate, peanut butter cups, and chocolate-covered caramels. We were very busy.

Deliveries

"I cannot believe we are almost finished," I said to Nannie. I was handing her yellow and lavender bows. She was wrapping the candy baskets in cellophane and tying them with the bows. I thought the candy baskets looked beautiful. So did everyone else in my big-house family.

Each basket for the hospital held real roses, chocolate leaves, and lots of chocolate candy, of course. Nannie had wrapped some of the candy in gold and purple foil. Ms. Colman's baskets were smaller. Nannie had wrapped Ms. Colman's candy in pink, green, and silver foil, and tied the baskets with green and pink ribbon. They looked soooo pretty.

"Ready for the deliveries, Karen?" asked Charlie. He picked up the baskets that were ready and started carrying them out to his car. "I think we are going to have to make a few trips," he said. "The Junk Bucket will not hold all these baskets."

"Do I have time to change?" I asked. I wanted to look my best when we delivered the baskets to the hospital and to Stoneybrook Manor.

Charlie looked at his watch. "I guess so," he said. "But do not take too long."

I handed the last bow to Nannie and rushed upstairs. My room was a mess, but that is nothing new. I found my blue velvet dress on the floor of my closet. My patent leather shoes were under the bed. I grabbed my white tights and a silver bracelet. When I was dressed, I brushed my hair and tied it back with a piece of navy ribbon that was on my desk. I thought I looked very grown-up.

"You look lovely," said Nannie when she saw me. "Thank you for all your help. I would never have been ready without you."

"Okay, Karen, let's go," said Charlie. "First stop, Stoneybrook General."

The hospital parking lot was very crowded. We unloaded the baskets and took them into the lobby. Lots of people told us how pretty they were.

"Thank you," I said politely. "I helped make them."

"Did you?" said a woman in a fur coat. I could tell she did not believe me. And that made me cross.

Luckily, the lady who was in charge of the dinner believed me. "You did a wonderful job. These baskets are beautiful," she said. She asked Charlie and me to place a basket at each big table in the hospital cafeteria. All the tables were set with white tablecloths and vases of flowers. Waiters with white aprons were carrying around silver trays

with glasses on them. I could smell delicious food cooking.

"Do we get to stay?" I asked hopefully.

"No," said Charlie, looking at his watch. "We have to deliver Ms. Colman's baskets, remember?"

Of course I remembered. It is just that I love parties, and I was all dressed up.

We did not get to stay at Ms. Colman's fund-raiser either. But I did see Ms. Colman. She was wearing a long navy blue velvet gown, sort of like my dress, only hers did not have lace at the collar or a sash. But it was very pretty.

"I love your baskets, Karen," said Ms. Colman. "Your grandmother told me how much you helped her with them. Thank you."

Feeling very proud, I drove home with Charlie.

Baskets for Everyone

"Here is the dark chocolate," I said to Nannie.

"Thank you, Karen," said Nannie as I handed it to her. I watched while she mixed dark and white chocolate together in the pan.

Nannie and I were very busy. It was the day after the fund-raisers, and guess what we were doing? Making candy for my class. Nannie was making swirly chocolate bars. (That was my name for them. They are bars of chocolate made from white, dark, and milk chocolate, all swirled together. Yum.)

We were making one basket for each group.

Here is what we put into the little baskets:

1. Chocolate cherries, peanut butter cups, fudge — all leftovers from the fund-raisers.

2. Swirly chocolate bars. Nannie made them especially for my class.

3. Lollipops. They were my idea.

When we were finished, we tied pink and green bows around the baskets.

The next day, I rode to school in the Junk Bucket with Charlie and Kristy — and the baskets, of course. Kristy helped me carry the baskets to my classroom.

"Finally," said Pamela when she saw us. But she was smiling. "I cannot wait to taste this candy," she told Kristy.

"They are here!" shouted Bobby when he saw the baskets.

"All right, class, please take your seats,"

said Ms. Colman when she came into the classroom. "I see Karen brought you wonderful candy. Everyone at the fund-raiser certainly enjoyed it."

"Can we eat the candy now?" begged Bobby.

Ms. Colman shook her head. In fact, my class had to wait until after social studies, math, spelling, and lunch before Ms. Colman let me pass out the baskets. I guess she did not want my class to ruin their appetites.

My friends took the baskets outside with them at recess. Instead of playing tag or hide-and-seek, we sat on benches and ate and talked, just like Pamela and her friends.

"These chocolate cherries are the best," said Bobby.

"I like the fudge," said Hank. (It was hard to understand him because his mouth was full.)

"I like everything," said Nancy.

"Me too," said Pamela as she munched on

a coconut bar. "Oh, Karen, you cannot go to Chicago. Who will bring us this great chocolate?"

"Yeah," said Hank.

"Try to stay," begged Ricky.

I looked at my classmates and felt as if I were going to cry. I was going to miss them if I moved.

Promises

"Have you decided whether you are moving, Karen?" asked Hannie. We were sitting together on the school bus, riding home.

I shook my head.

"Have you talked to Andrew?"

"No," I said. "But I will." I looked out the window and sighed.

Hannie sighed too. "I wish you would stay here in Stoneybrook. You promised you would try."

"I know," I said.

*   *   *

When I jumped off the bus, I saw Andrew in the backyard playing catch with David Michael. I thought about my promise to him — that we would stay together, no matter what. I knew that meant I should move to Chicago, but I was not sure I wanted to go. And I had promised Hannie and Nancy I would try to stay.

I picked a daisy. "I leave. I stay," I chanted as I pulled off the petals one by one. "I stay," I said as I threw the last petal on the ground. Hmmm.

"Hi, Karen," said Andrew then.

"Hi," I replied. I waved to Andrew and David Michael. Then I went in the house and up to my room. (I did not even stop in the kitchen to say hello to Nannie.) I needed to think.

I sat on the bed and told Moosie about my promise to Andrew. And my promise to my friends. He did not know what I should do either.

I thought about what promises mean,

that when you say you will do something, you have to do it if that is what you promised. I thought about all the promises I had made lately. I promised my class candy. I promised Nannie I would help her. I promised Hannie and Nancy I would try to stay in Stoneybrook. But my biggest promise of all had been to Andrew. I sighed. Luckily I did not have to decide about Chicago right away. But I did know one thing. I had kept some hard promises. And now I might have to break one.

I did not want to break a promise.

About the Author

ANN M. MARTIN lives in New York City and loves animals, especially cats. She has two cats of her own, Gussie and Woody.

Other books by Ann M. Martin that you might enjoy are *Stage Fright*; *Me and Katie (the Pest)*; and the books in *The Baby-sitters Club* series.

Ann likes ice cream and *I Love Lucy*. And she has her own little sister, whose name is Jane.

Little Sister

Don't miss #96

KAREN'S BIG MOVE

"Daddy," I said, "I have something to tell you. I have decided what I will do. I am going to move to Chicago with Mommy and Seth and Andrew."

At first Daddy did not answer. "I am sorry to hear that," he said at last. "You know that we will all miss you."

"I will miss you very much too," I said. "That is why it was so hard for me to make my decision. But I will be back in six months."

"Karen," said Daddy. "I am glad you finally figured out what it is you want to do. But if you change your mind for any reason, do not forget what we decided. You can always come back to the big house. Your mom and I do not want you to be miserable."

"Thank you, Daddy," I said.

Little Sister

by Ann M. Martin
author of The Baby-sitters Club®

More Titles... ➡

Available wherever you buy books, or use this order form.

Scholastic Inc., P.O. Box 7502, Jefferson City, MO 65102

Please send me the books I have checked above. I am enclosing $_____ (please add $2.00 to cover shipping and handling). Send check or money order – no cash or C.O.Ds please.

Name_____Birthdate_____

–

Address_____

–

City_____State/Zip_____